A gift for

Lucy

from
Teah's Mummy
Debbie
"Merry Christmas 2008"

An Aussie Day Before Christmas

For all the helpers of furry creatures
at *wires.org.au*

Scholastic Press
345 Pacific Highway Lindfield NSW 2070
An imprint of Scholastic Australia Pty Limited (ABN 11 000 614 577)
PO Box 579 Gosford NSW 2250
www.scholastic.com.au

Part of the Scholastic Group
Sydney · Auckland · New York · Toronto · London · Mexico City · New Delhi · Hong Kong · Buenos Aires · Puerto Rico

First published by Scholastic Australia in 2008.
Text and illustrations copyright © Kilmeny Niland, 2008.
www.kilmenyniland.com

The National Library of Australia Cataloguing-in-Publication entry
Author: Niland, Kilmeny.
Title: Aussie day before Christmas / author, Kilmeny Niland.
Publisher: Gosford, N.S.W. : Scholastic Press, 2008.
ISBN: 9781741690972 (hbk.)
Target Audience: For children.
Dewey Number: A823.3

Typeset in Aperto.

Printed by Tien Wah Press, Malaysia.

10 9 8 7 6 5 4 3 2 1   89 / 012

An Aussie Day Before Christmas

Kilmeny Niland

A Scholastic Press book • Scholastic Australia

'Twas the day before Christmas
and in his beach shack,
Santa was snoozing
flat out on his back.

'Shake a leg, love,'
Sheila Claus said.
'Time to get ready
for the big night ahead.'

Santa yawned and turned over
and mumbled, 'Mmmm . . . no . . .'
then suddenly twigged,
'Oi, it's Chrissy! Ho Ho!'

As he pulled on his shorts
and his old singlet too,
he said 'Let's get crackin'!'
to his trusty mate, Blue.

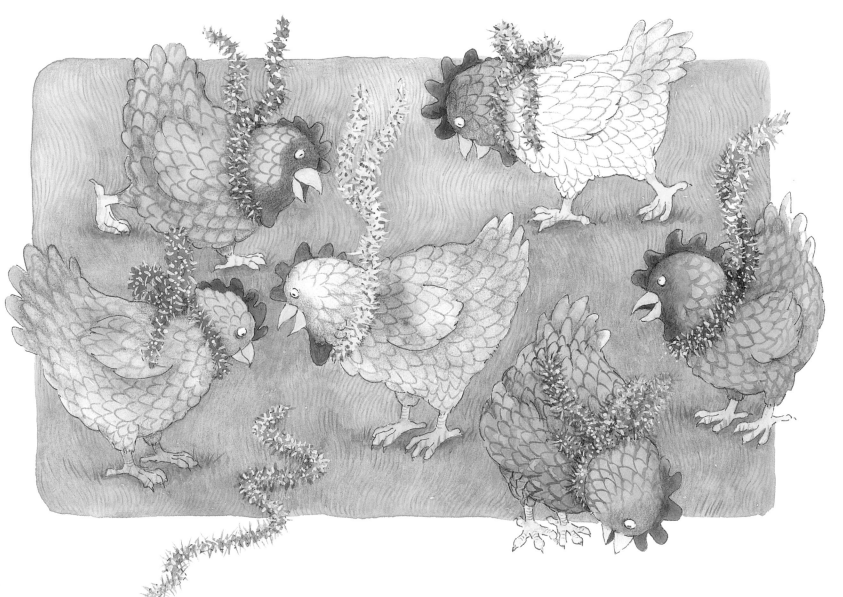

'The chooks need some tucker,
my tum's rumblin' too;
I need help baggin' prezzies,
then we'll sort out those 'roos.'

He wolfed down his brekkie
of snags, toast and honey;
took a walk with his missus,
read the news in the dunny.

Santa searched for his helpers—
'Buzzin' blowies—they're like!
The day I need help,
they're on flamin' strike!'

But behind the shed doors,
piled high in the ute,
he saw mountains of prezzies.
Santa twinkled, 'You beaut!'

Then he whistled the 'roos,
'Cooeeeeee, hop along,'
but only cicadas
chiacked with their song.

Santa was cranky.
'We need 'roos for the show.
The koalas won't help me,
they're too flamin' slow.'

High in a gum tree,
a kooka was looking.
'Crikey, Raelene,
can you tell us what's cookin'?'

She flapped off at once
like the flick of a whip,
flew back with the news—
they were having a kip.

She started to laugh
with her mates joining in.
Santa thumped on a drum.
Oi! What a din!

In all shapes and sizes,
'roos crashed through the bush.
They hopped, jumped and bounded,
'til Santa yelled, 'Shooosh!'

'Hey, Bruce, how ya goin'?
And Stace, that's a load.
G'day, Daz and Tezza!
We need eight for the road.

'From Woy Woy to Woop Woop,
Aussie kids are excited.
I reckon by mornin'
they'll be deadset delighted.'

The 'roos queued in twos from biggest to smallest
so Santa could choose the strongest and tallest,
to pull the old ute and whizz through the night
with sacks full of prezzies on this once-a-year flight.

Eight 'roos were soon harnessed
amid Aussie salutes,
while others were nosing
their lolly-bag loot.

'Now, let's have a cuppa.
I'd better eat light,
to keep heaps of room
for those goodies—too right!'

With a squizz at his clobber
to choose what to wear,
he grabbed a grouse shirt,
then brylcreamed his hair.

At last he was ready,
gave his missus a squeeze.
'Seeya later,' said Sheila.
'Drive carefully, please!'

Dusk was now falling,
so Santa and Blue
swept away with a wheelie . . .